Found

JOSEPH BRUCHAC

7th Generation
SUMMERTOWN, TENNESSEE

Library of Congress Cataloging-in-Publication Data is available on request.

We chose to print this title on paper certified by The Forest Stewardship Council® (FSC®), a global, not-for-profit organization dedicated to the promotion of responsible forest management worldwide.

MIX
Paper from
responsible sources
FSC
www.fsc.org FSC® C005010

Cover and interior design: John Wincek

7th Generation
Book Publishing Company
PO Box 99, Summertown, TN 38483
888-260-8458
bookpubco.com
nativevoicesbooks.com

ISBN: 978-1-939053-23-7

25 24 23 22 21 20   1 2 3 4 5 6 7 8 9

Contents

CHAPTER 1 **Don't Sit Still** 1

CHAPTER 2 **Stay Calm** 5

CHAPTER 3 **A List** 11

CHAPTER 4 **A Plan** 15

CHAPTER 5 **Shelter** 21

CHAPTER 6 **Fire** 25

CHAPTER 7 **First Morning** 33

CHAPTER 8 **Climbing** 39

CHAPTER 9 **The Sound of the Copter** . . . 47

CHAPTER 10 **The Riverbank Cave** 53

CHAPTER 11 **The Roar** 59

CHAPTER 12 **Bear Song** 63

CHAPTER 13 **Going Slow** 69

CHAPTER 14 **Ferns** 75

CHAPTER 15 **They Don't Know Me** 83

CHAPTER 16 **The Copter** 87

CHAPTER 17 **Curiosity** 93

CHAPTER 18 **Found** 97

About the Author 107

*To my son James Bruchac
and my good friend John Stokes
—real-life trackers and wilderness teachers.*

Don't Sit Still

Sit still.

That's usually the first rule when you're lost. Start wandering around and you'll just get more lost. Stay where you are. Then it's more likely someone will find you.

But what if you're not really lost? What if you don't want to be found? What if being found means something a whole lot worse than being lost? What then?

Nick looked around. The stream in front of him seemed to be running from east to west toward the distant ocean. The train trestle in front of him was going north to south. High overhead, it arced like a steel rainbow between the two tunnels bored into the mountains.

But that was nearly all he knew about where he was. Except that he was somewhere between the place he'd left and the place he was going. And that he was in a wilderness area with forests and mountains all around him. He was also far from the nearest train station. How far? He wasn't sure how long he'd been on the train before he was pushed off it.

Two hours? Three? He looked at his wristwatch. He observed where the sun was in the sky. It was still a long way from sunset. Exactly how long? It was hard to tell this time of year. This far north the days were very long at this time of year.

He'd never made this trip before, so nothing—including the trestle—looked familiar.

He could climb back up. It wouldn't be easy, but his arms were strong enough and his balance was good. Heights didn't bother him. He was a competent rock climber.

Get up there, then follow the tracks backward through the tunnel to an open area, and then wait for the next train. There weren't that many. He'd looked at the schedule before getting on the train. There was one every twelve hours either going north or heading south. He could wait that long.

But so could the muscular bald man who'd shoved him out the door. He might on that train heading south. Or someone who'd been given his description might be on the northbound express. Not that a description was necessary. How many brown-skinned teenagers with a brush cut were likely to be standing by a train track in the middle of nowhere?

Nick felt as if a fist was clenched inside his chest. His hands were shaking.

Sit down. Breathe. Calm down. That was what Grampa Elie always said.

There was a big rock next to the small river. Its sides were smooth from thousands of years of water washing over it. The top of the stone was flat, shaped as if it had been made for sitting.

Nick shrugged the pack off his back and sat.

He felt himself calming down. The adrenaline was working its way out of his system.

He ran his palms over the tough canvas of the old backpack.

"Thank you," he said to it.

Nick had always been quiet. He preferred listening to talking. According to what his parents told him, he hadn't really started talking until he was almost three years old.

But saying thank you to his pack was the right thing to do now. It had saved his life. One of its straps had caught on a spike sticking out from the rail tie as he fell. It had stopped his fall.

That was good luck.

But the man who'd thrown him off the train had seen the pack save him. He'd been leaning over the railing at the back of the train. Just before the train disappeared into the mouth of the tunnel, that man smiled, showing his teeth. Then he made a gesture. He drew his finger across his throat and pointed at Nick.

That was bad luck.

Stay Calm

I *need to stay calm,* Nick told himself. *Fear is the mind-killer.* That was what Grampa Elie told Nick when Nick was only seven.

"Abenaki saying?" Nick had asked.

"Nah, it's from one of my favorite books, *Dune.* Read it, Nosi. It's a classic."

So Nick had done just that. Even at the age of seven he loved reading. And Grampa Elie was right. The book was awesome. Then he'd seen the movies based on the book. But the book was better.

Grampa Elie hadn't been surprised when Nick told him he preferred the book.

"Pictures are better when you make them in your mind," he'd said. "Reading makes you think. Thinking's always a good thing. Even when you're scared, don't ever stop thinking."

Grampa Elie had been a Ranger in Vietnam. He was at a base called Khe Sanh when it was suddenly attacked from all sides at night. Unlike most everyone else, Elie St. Francis had kept thinking, stayed calm, and stayed alive.

"A lot of those other guys," he told Nick, "were running around like chickens with their heads cut off. 'Get down, get behind something,'" I told them. "'Pick up your gun. Start shooting back. The enemy's that way. Pay attention.'"

Nick hadn't been paying attention. He'd just been feeling fortunate that he'd been able to catch a train a day earlier than his itinerary. No one would be waiting at the station on the other end until Friday. And he'd been smiling at the thought of how he would be able to make his way to Camp Seven Generations, where he'd be teaching woodcraft to other Native kids a few years younger than him from several First Nations communities. He'd get there so much earlier that no one would be expecting him yet. He'd stalk up on the place and observe everyone while staying hidden in the brush. Then, when they'd least expect it, he'd walk into the mess hall in time for dinner and tease people gently for not having guessed he was anywhere around. *Didn't any of you feel like you were being watched?* It could be his first lesson for them on awareness.

But Nick was so lost in imagining what he'd do that he was unaware himself. What was it that his first martial arts teacher had told him?

When a wise man starts congratulating himself, he becomes a fool. That was the reason he'd ended up this way. Maybe, too, it was because he was thinking about what he'd overheard in the dining car. Some of the other Native people in the dining car were talking about oil. They'd talked about how there was a big push to open up the reserves to oil exploration and how the people were going to resist it just like the Mi'qmaq did a few years ago over in Nova Scotia.

For whatever reason, he hadn't watched where he was going. Coming back from the dining car, he'd turned right instead of left and entered the wrong train car thinking it was his. Another reason was that the train was an old one, so old that some of the locks on the sleeping compartment doors didn't work. That was why he was able to open the wrong door, and why he saw the bald man on the floor.

Garrote.

That was the name for the thing the bald man in the black T-shirt was using. It was a length of piano wire with a piece of wood fastened on either end. It was wrapped around the throat of the man being held facedown by the bald man's right knee. The muscles on the bald man's arms were bulging as he pulled. A thin red line of blood was showing where the wire crossed his victim's throat.

Nick saw it all in less time that it would take to count from one to three. But it felt like an eternity. It was as if everything was in slow motion. He was frozen, with his fingers grasping the door handle, his eyes taking in everything in the compartment. He didn't just see the two men on the floor. He also saw the open suitcase on the bed, the brown briefcase decorated with beadwork next to the window, and the victim's rimless eyeglasses on the floor by the right knee of the man pulling back on the garrote.

A cascade of thoughts went through his mind.

That guy's dead. Is he Chinese? He is so dead. Back up. Shut the door. Say something. Say I didn't see anything? Back up. Shut the door.

Then the bald man lifted his head toward Nick. He didn't seem shocked. He didn't seem upset. He looked up with eyes as black and cold and emotionless and dead as the water of a deep well. Then he smiled and nodded.

Nick knew what that meant. He spun around, banging the pack on his back into the wall of the narrow corridor. As he reached the end of the car, he heard a sound behind him. A compartment door was being shut.

As soon as he entered the next car, he knew he'd gone the wrong way. The car was empty. All the other passengers were in the front cars. He was at the end of the train.

Before he could turn, a hand slapped him on his back, pushing him against the wall. Two arms were wrapped around him. A bald head was pressed against the back of his neck so that Nick couldn't try to throw his own head back and hit the man in his face. Then he was shoved through the back door of the train car.

He was held there for a moment, with his feet lifted above the floor of the platform. He tried to kick, to break free. The bald man's arms were like iron bands. Nick felt as helpless as a kitten. He'd been taught ways to fight back, but none of them would work when he was pinned tight like this. It was dark all around them. The rattle and roar of the train was deafening. They were in a tunnel.

Suddenly there was light everywhere. They'd come out onto a high trestle between the two tunnels bored into the ancient living rock.

"Excellent!"

The bald man's voice in his ear was calm. Even before he was hoisted up higher, Nick knew what the bald assassin had decided to do to him.

Am I going to die? he'd thought.

"It's just business, kid. No hard feelings." There was no more emotion in his voice than if he'd been apologizing for bumping into someone in the street. Just for a second, as the man tossed him spinning over the railing, Nick found himself looking into the bald man's eyes. Again, he saw they were as black as the water in a deep well, emotionless and dead.

And then Nick felt himself falling.

A List

Nick felt his heart beginning to speed up again at the memory of how close he'd come to dying.

It's okay to be upset, he said to himself. *After all, someone just tried to kill me. Acknowledge it. Accept it. Then get on with it. Do what I need to do.*

He thought about the lecture he had been planning to give the junior high kids at Camp Seven Generations where he'd been heading:

When you're trying to survive, what's most important? Nope, not food.

Number One: Air. Without air, you'll be dead in minutes.

Number Two: Shelter. If you're stuck out in the sun, you'll get heat stroke. If you're too cold, you'll get hypothermia. Even when it's not freezing cold, you can get hypothermia if you just get wet and don't dry yourself off. So you need shelter.

Number Three: Fire, if it's cold. But you can survive in a brush shelter or a snow cave with no fire.

Number Four: Water. You can go for a couple of days with no water, but can't go that long if you're in a desert.

Number Five: Food. You can last a week or two without eating.

What do I have in my pack? Nick thought.

He hardly had to ask himself that. After all, he'd packed it himself. When he traveled, he always kept it close. That was why he had it on his back when he returned from the dining car. He was pretty sure he knew the contents by heart. But pretty sure isn't good enough when your life depends on it. How many times are people pretty sure they have something with them and then find out they don't?

Nick pulled his pack up into his lap. It wasn't one of the new state-of-the-art backpacks made of nylon, with a lightweight frame and all sorts of watertight zipper pockets. It was made of canvas. Faded khaki green. Old, but tough.

"It's tough like me, Nosi," Grampa Elie had said when he gave it to Nick.

Nosi. That means "grandson" in the Abenaki language. Nick loved it when Grampa Elie called him that.

"Saved my life," his grandfather had continued. He'd pointed at an unmended hole in the side of the pack. "Bullet went right in there, where I had stowed my lighter. Hit so hard it knocked me down, but all I got was a bruise on my shoulder blade."

Nick ran his hand across the pack. *A lifesaver, for sure*, he thought. He opened the straps. He pulled out the waterproof inner bag, unzipped it, and reached inside.

He carefully laid each item on the flat boulder. First was his sheathed knife. It was on top because it was the only thing he had to put into his regular luggage when he flew. Ten inches long with a five-inch blade, it would have been taken at the first security check. Next was his compass, wrapped in a red bandanna. Then a warm, waterproof, hooded jacket that folded up small and weighed almost nothing.

Item by item he took everything else out. Cotton socks. Three pairs. Two extra undershorts. A three-meters-long roll of cord. His first aid kit. A ziplock bag of rations that held several big handfuls of shelled nuts and broken-up chocolate bars, as well as three wrapped energy bars. Three water-filtration straws. An empty, lightweight canteen. A map of the Canadian province he was in. The two watertight tins. One held the emergency kit. The other held his fire-making things. His ID was in the small wallet that also contained a single credit card and $200. There was also a roll of toilet paper in a ziplock bag. It was the one luxury he allowed himself when roughing it. Dry leaves just didn't do the trick.

Everything he'd placed in the bag was spread out in front of him. And that, aside from what he was wearing, was all he had. His bigger backpack was still in his sleeping compartment. So was his cell phone—plugged in to recharge it.

But he had enough. More than enough. The old nineteenth-century naturalist John Muir had hiked all over America, supposedly with only a change of underwear in his bag. Then there was that big guy in those novels he loved—the former Army MP who carried nothing but a toothbrush. It wasn't just what you had that counted. It was what you did with it. And what counted even more was what you carried in the one place no one else could see—your mind.

A Plan

ow Nick had to make a plan. Especially since this wasn't like the usual survival scenario. It wasn't just a question of surviving until he could find his way out or be found. If he was found—by the wrong person or people—he'd be like that poor Asian guy who got garroted.

Ten to one Dead Eyes carried the murdered guy's body back through that empty last car. Then he tossed the corpse off the train on some remote stretch. He'd probably cleaned up the scene to leave no trace. Except there was one problem. One brown-skinned kid with a brush cut who'd seen what happened and had seen his face. A loose end that needed to be tied off.

Nick sat down and unzipped his hooded jacket. Its lining made it almost too warm, but it would be welcome if the nights got cold. He wiped his palms on his jeans. Not the trendy, preworn jeans with holes in them—just thick, sturdy denim. Then he spread the provincial map—which was coated with waterproof plastic—out on top of a rock and studied it. The rail line was marked on it, as were the rivers and streams that it crossed. With the elevation markers on the map, Nick had a general idea of where he was. There would be no roads—just mountains and streams to cross and days of travel. It was not an area with popular hiking trails. But if he did things right, he could find his way and reach the nearest First Nations reserve fifty miles to the east. It would be safer heading there than going north to the camp where he'd been hired as a summer survival instructor.

Why not go to that original destination?

There was a good chance that Dead Eyes had figured out where Nick was going. All the man had to do was go back one car past the dining car to find the room with Nick's bigger bag in it. Going through it, he'd learn Nick's name, where he was from, and his destination, if he didn't just get all that info and more from the unlocked phone Nick had left behind.

Nick carefully put everything except the knife and one spare pair of socks back in the same order he took it out. Routine. *Routine is your friend.* He strapped the knife onto his belt and shouldered his pack.

He looked at the stream flowing down through the valley below the trestle.

Great.

He began to walk along the water, heading downstream. West. As he went he left footprints every now and then—not too many, but enough—in the pockets of yellow sand along its edge. He scuffed the moss on top of one stone and broke a low-hanging branch fifty yards farther down. Where the valley widened out half a mile or so farther, he turned and headed south into the woods. As he did so, he left a few footprints and more "accidentally" bent or broken branches as markers. He stopped when he came to a wide ledge of bare rock. A good place for the false trail to end.

Let Dead Eyes and whoever else might come looking for me follow this, he thought.

Then, taking great care to leave no signs of his passing, he walked back to the stream, balancing himself on top of stones. He stepped into the shallow water and began to go east. He passed again under the trestle, past the wide, flat boulder. Half an hour later, he left the water. The trestle was three turns in the little river behind him.

Nick looked over yet another smooth stone before sitting on it. No worries about poisonous snakes this far north, but there were still insects and spiders and centipedes to think about. And ants. Nick loved reading things about nature and memorizing them. The total weight of all the ants in the world was either equal to or more than the total weight of all the humans. Ants were on every continent except Antarctica, although there were cockroaches in the warm buildings humans placed there. None of the ants in Canada were really dangerous to people. They were not like the driver ants of the tropics—which could ooze acid out of their jaws—but being overly cautious was better than regretting being careless.

He unlaced his boots and slid them off. They weren't new. Only an idiot or someone in love with blisters would set out on a journey in new boots. But they were sturdy and made of good leather that had been worn in, so those boots both fit snugly and gave where give was needed.

His socks seemed dry. The boots had not soaked through, and he'd been careful not to step into any deep places where the water would come over their tops. But just to make sure, he put the socks he'd just taken off into a side pouch in his pack. To cool off his feet, he sat barefoot for a few minutes before putting on the clean socks and his boots. He took the canteen from his pack and knelt by the stream. Facing the mouth of the canteen downstream, he filled it where the water was running swiftest over the rocks.

Then, compass in hand, he left the stream to head east through the forest.

Without a compass it might have been hard for some people to keep in a straight line. But Nick only glanced at it now and then. Mostly he used the method Grampa Elie had taught him. Line up four trees in a row at least a hundred yards apart. Then go from tree one to tree two to tree three to tree four. Look back, get your line, and then choose four more trees ahead of you.

Nick moved at an even pace. Not running, but not walking either.

It wasn't hard to navigate through the tall trees—coast redwoods, most of them. They weren't virgin timber. None of the trees were the giants that were here before white men started logging. But the last time this area had been cut had certainly been decades ago. The undergrowth was not difficult to get through. A natural fire—likely set off by lightning—had been through and burned up the smaller fallen limbs, the dry brush, and the berry bushes. So it was easy to get sight lines and to move without pushing through heavy undergrowth or, worse, blackberry tangles. Now and then there was a long, low hump grown over with moss across his way. It was all that was left of a big tree that had fallen a long time ago. Everything around him was shades of green and gray—old man's beard moss hanging from the lower limbs, lichen on the bases of the tree roots. It wasn't quite as moist as the northern rain-forest woodlands of the Pacific Coast where he'd spent days doing wilderness camping. But everything around him glowed with the kind of life that regular rains bring. There'd be no problem about finding drinkable water.

The land began to rise steeply in front of him. He was at the base of the first of the ridges shown on his map. After three hours of steady travel, he'd covered about seven miles. From here on, as he climbed, it would be slower.

And colder. The top of the ridge, perhaps a mile away, was white with snow.

Not a good idea to climb that ridge now. It was 7:00 p.m. by his watch, and the sun would be out of sight by the time he reached that ridgetop.

It had been a warm day—warm enough that he'd sweated a little as he'd jogged along. But he could already feel things starting to cool down. All of his heavier clothing was in the bag left behind on the train. He'd need to make a shelter for the night.

Shelter

There was a small rise in front of Nick. It looked perfect. It was the kind of place that would not flood if there was a heavy rain. He walked to the top, where there was a level area about half the size of a small bedroom. He knelt and pressed his hand on the ground. The earth was dry.

He stood and faced first one direction and then another, making a circle as slowly as if he was doing tai chi. The air was still. No wind was blowing. But that could change at any minute. From west to east was the usual way the wind blew. He looked at the trees around him. The larger ones were spruce and fir trees—evergreens mixed with birch, beech, and maple. The taller evergreens were all bent near the top in the same direction. That was from being pushed by the wind. Pushed from west to east.

That meant he should build his shelter so that its opening faced the east. You don't want the wind blowing into your face. Wind blowing in makes it hard to stay warm. Rain gets blown in too. And if you make a fire in front of your shelter, the choking smoke will be pushed inside. Plus, facing east means catching the first rays of the sun in the morning.

Always look up before you decide on a spot to stay.

Nick looked up as he turned in a circle the second time. No dead trees or limbs were close by his little hilltop. That was one of the dangers of spending the night in the woods. More than one person had gotten badly hurt or even died when a tree or a branch fell on them. It didn't take that big of a branch, either. One the size of a baseball bat could break your limbs.

But there were lots of fallen branches of various sizes under nearby trees. Perfect sizes, in fact. He walked down off the rise and began to sort through them. He set aside three relatively straight and smooth poles and brought them back up to the hilltop. Two were about six feet long. The third was close to ten feet.

The earth itself would be his mattress. But he didn't want to roll over in the night onto a sharp twig. So he set his lodge poles aside, knelt, and brushed the ground free of sticks and leaves where the floor of his lean-to would be. For a more permanent structure, he might have made a bed from green boughs and woven them together the way Cree people did when they set up hunting camps. That would make a springy, good-smelling floor that could be used for weeks. Now, though, for two reasons, that would not be a good idea. First, it would be wasteful. Sure, he'd thank any tree he cut a branch from. But why hurt a tree when he didn't need to? Second, and more important, he wanted to leave as little trace of himself as possible.

Using some of the cord in his pack, he tied the two six-footers together at the top. Then he attached the third pole so they formed an A-frame, about four feet high in the front and sloping to the ground in the back. He used slipknots that would hold firm but be quick and easy to untie.

A Canada jay flew down to land on a branch overhead as he worked.

Wisakedjak, Nick thought. *That's what the Cree people call you.*

The bird looked at Nick, staring at him with one eye. It was so comical that it made Nick laugh.

It kept looking at him.

All right, Nick thought.

He opened his pack and took out a few of the shelled nuts. Placing them on his right palm, he held his hand out toward the bird. It cocked its head and made a wheet-wheet call. Then it flew down and landed on his wrist. It picked up the nuts, one after another, before spreading its wings.

Nick felt some of the tension in his chest let go as the jay flew away. It was as if it had come to reassure him. In Cree stories, Wisakedjak was a trickster, but it was also a friend of humans.

I'm going to be okay, Nick thought as he went back down the hill to gather more branches, shorter ones this time.

Again, it didn't take long before he had a large stack of dead limbs. He sorted them into two piles. The driest ones were for firewood. The others, straight sticks ranging from five or six feet to two feet in length, were for the framework.

He began to lean them against the sides of his A-frame. Lots of them so they filled in the lean-to's skeleton. Of course, there were still gaps between the side branches. But when he piled on armfuls of moss and fallen fir boughs, the gaps disappeared. He looked again at his watch. Not yet 8:00 p.m. Building his shelter had taken less than half an hour.

There was still an hour before full dark would settle in. Time to make a fire.

Fire

Nick scraped the leaves and needles off the ground in front of the opening to his shelter. He kept on doing this until he cleared everything away in the shape of a circle four feet wide. Using his knife, he cut up pieces of mossy earth, leaving a smaller circle of sand exposed for a fire pit. There were loose rocks around the hill next to him. He gathered a dozen and placed them around the fire pit. Not all the way around. He left the partial circle of stones open toward his shelter. Then he placed the pieces of mossy earth behind the rocks. They would help keep a fire from spreading.

Most important thing about a fire, Nosi, is to get it ready right.

Nick smiled to himself. Whenever he was getting set to make a fire, he'd always hear those words. Grampa Elie had first said them to him when Nick was only four years old.

He placed down several heavier sticks, each about a foot long, to make a base for the fire. He'd gathered some paper-dry bark from the birch trees, stripping it from dead fallen limbs. Perfect.

Birch, thank you, Nick thought as he tore the bark into strips that coiled as he tore them off. *You covered our lodges. You gave yourself to make our canoes. You are one of our oldest friends.*

The Abenaki name for "birch" means "blanket tree." One of the stories Aunt Marge told him was about a little girl who had gotten lost in the woods. Her parents couldn't find her, even though they looked and looked. It was getting cold and snow was starting. They were afraid she'd freeze. But the next morning, when they found her, she was just fine. She had wrapped a big piece of birch bark around herself and stayed warm.

After Nick had a big enough pile, he began propping up thin twigs in a tipi shape around the birch strips. Then he made a second layer of larger dry sticks over the twigs. Patiently and carefully, he built up his fire tipi until it was about eighteen inches high. Too big and a fire is wasteful or even dangerous.

Nick shook his head as he thought of the story he'd seen a year or two ago on his iPhone's news feed. Some guy had tried to imitate something he'd seen on a TV show about forging your own sword. He'd made a huge fire in an oil barrel, and it got away from him. That fire ended up burning down a whole neighborhood, and the man ended up in jail.

Nick sat down cross-legged between the fire pit and his shelter. He knew a lot of ways to start a fire, ways that he was prepared to teach the campers at that school where he'd been heading. Fire plow, hand drill and bow drill, flint and steel, focusing the sunlight through a magnifying glass, and using a cigarette lighter or touching a 9-volt battery to steel wool. You could even— if you were really desperate or sick of hearing from telemarketers—cut into the side of your cell phone to expose the lithium battery, which would burst into flame when exposed to air.

Mentioning that last method always got a few horrified gasps from kids and some knowing smiles from grown-ups. But Nick had no intention of doing any of those things. He took the tightly sealed round pillbox out of one of the small plastic bags in his pack. He removed a single safety match and replaced the top on the pillbox, which he'd wrapped with striking paper. He leaned close to the fire tipi and reached in, striking the match next to the tinder. The birch bark lit right away with an almost smokeless flame. He'd left plenty of gaps between the piled sticks of the fire tipi so the fire was quickly getting all the air it needed. No need to blow on it as you do when starting your fire from a single coal packed with a bow drill and placed into a tinder bundle.

Nick sat back and stowed his matches in his pack, which he then placed behind him in the lean-to. The entire fire tipi was burning now. He'd done a good job selecting dry branches. He had wood placed around his fire pit to feed the fire after it was started. Enough wood to keep a small, warm fire going all night.

He began to put some of those larger pieces of wood onto the fire, crisscrossing them. He did that very carefully so he didn't smother the flames.

Take care of a fire when it's little, and it will take care of you when its big.

Some of the branches he'd gathered were thicker than his arm and six or eight feet long. He hadn't bothered trying to break them up into smaller lengths. When the fire was hot enough, he put the ends of three of them into the fire. Now all he had to do was push them farther into the fire as they burned through the night.

The warmth of the fire felt good on his face. He was feeling thirsty, though. He uncapped his canteen and took a slow drink. He'd already put a water-purifying tablet into it. Even though he was fairly certain that the stream wasn't contaminated, it was better to be safe than sorry. Even ponds and rivers far from so-called civilization often had microscopic organisms that caused beaver fever.

It was dark now. A few bright stars could be seen through the trees, but the moon had yet to show her face. The fire made him feel not just warm but also secure. It was an old way to feel, a way people had felt thousands and thousands of years ago when their fires protected them from the giant animals that hunted human beings back then.

Those huge bears and saber-toothed cats were long gone now. True, there were mountain lions and bears—maybe even some grizzlies—in this part of the continent. But those weren't usually a danger. They tended to be more afraid of people than people needed to be afraid of them. And a fire would warn them off. There were wolves, but no Native person was ever worried about them. They were just big, wild canines, not that far removed from dogs. All those stories about wolves attacking people were folk tales from European people.

People, Nick thought. *People are what's most dangerous.*

The image of the calm, brutal face of the man he thought of as Dead Eyes came back into his memory. A shiver went down his back. Then he pushed it aside, remembering again something Grampa Elie had said.

Don't worry about what you can't change. Just be prepared to do what you can when you need to do it.

He walked a few yards downwind and pried a shovel-shaped piece of wood from an old stump. He carefully dug a shallow pit latrine, an outdoor toilet, putting the dirt aside on top of a wide, flat piece of bark so that it could easily be put back into the hole.

Nick thought about a poem he'd read once by a Cherokee writer named Smoke Arnett. It spoke about how you can judge a creature by the amount of scat they leave behind for others to see.

When Nick was done, he filled the latrine back in, scattering leaves and twigs and needles on top of where the hole had been. He stepped back and nodded. It all blended in. No sign any human had been there. The old Cherokee poet would have been pleased.

Nick walked back to his fire. On his way, he used his knife to cut a green twig from a beech sapling and stripped the bark off it with his fingernail. Then he slid down in front of the fire. He put a few more pieces of wood into it and leaned forward, his elbows on his knees. He sat there for quite a while, just looking into the fire's flames, enjoying the changing colors and dancing patterns, feeling the comfort of warmth and light.

You're never alone when you have a fire.

The dark forest around him felt peaceful. But it wasn't quiet. There was rustling in the leaves. Shrews and mice. And from the distance came the hoo-hoo, hoo-hoo-hoo call of a barred owl.

Nick reached into his pack to scoop a small handful of his trail mix from the bag. He picked out a few pieces of almond and tossed them out beyond the light of his fire.

"I share my food with you, little sisters and brothers," he said in a soft voice.

He put the rest of the handful into his mouth and chewed it slowly, enjoying every bit of it, from the sweetness of the chocolate to the crunchiness of the nuts. He took a gulp of water from his canteen, swishing it around in his mouth before swallowing. Then, after grinding the end of the beech twig between his molars, he used it as a brush to clean his teeth.

The stars were less bright now through the trees. The full moon's calm face was up there, her gentle light filling the sky.

"Good night, Grandmother," Nick whispered.

Then he slid into the lean-to. Using his tightly closed pack as a pillow, he lay back. Something stuck into the center of his back, probably a small stone that he'd somehow missed. Rather than trying to find it, he just rolled onto his side. Curled up facing the fire, he closed his eyes and slept.

First Morning

hough he'd added wood twice during the night, Nick's fire was out when he woke. It didn't matter. It had kept him warm during the coolest part of the night. However, his head seemed a little stuffed up and his sense of smell seemed to have been dulled. Congested. Not from sleeping out, though. His throat had felt a little sore when he was on the train. Probably something he'd picked up from other people— one of those late-summer head colds.

Sometime, maybe later in the day, he'd have to find a pine tree. Pine needles steeped in boiling water make a great tea, one that's good for colds and sore throats.

The first light of the sun was showing over the top of the ridge. The sounds of birdsong were echoing through the trees. Nick smiled. It was always good to be where what he heard was not city sounds, or any human noises at all—just the ancient, joyous dawn chorus welcoming a new day.

He wasn't sure he recognized the voices of any of the unseen singers. Being from the northeast, he didn't know many of the native birds found in this part of Canada. But he heard a warbling song that had to be from some sort of thrush. Swainson's, maybe? It was followed by a clear whistling call, a sort of turr-teet tee-tee-tee tee-tee-tee tee-tee-tee that might be a white-throated sparrow.

Then, with a flutter of its wings and a soft caw, a Canada jay dropped down to land right on the ground in front of him. Probably the same bird he'd seen the evening before, and likely one of this year's new additions to the forest. Unlike a lot of other birds, Canada jays lay their eggs and make their nests in the coldest part of the winter. And in the summer, when their little ones become large enough, they are sent out to be on their own for a while until they can form a family of their own.

"More?" Nick asked.

The small gray bird opened its wings slightly and bobbed its head up and down.

Nick picked several pieces of almonds from his trail mix and held them out on his palm. The jay hopped up onto his thumb, took the pieces of nut one by one, and then flew off.

If I wasn't worried about being followed, Nick thought, *this would be a good place to spend more than one day.*

He ate a handful of his trail mix and drank from his canteen. Then he took out one of his energy bars. He'd made them himself, wrapping each bar in waxed paper so there would be no plastic waste. He shook his head thinking of how often, even in what seemed remote wilderness, he'd find human garbage left behind. Gum and candy wrappers, bottles and cans, and drink containers of all kinds, along with cigarette filters, plastic bags, straws, socks, hats, gloves, and other articles of clothing he'd rather not think about. Nick would use a stick to pick up the items and put them in the garbage bag he always had with him. People either never heard—or maybe didn't care—about that old rule: *If you carry it in, carry it out again.*

So Nick would pick that stuff up. Sometimes— after hiking some trails in the Adirondacks or the Green Mountains—Nick ended up carrying out twice as much as he'd carried in.

He folded the waxed paper up and tucked it back into his pack. The paper would burn clean— part of the tinder for his next fire.

Then he checked his fire circle from the night before.

Never leave a fire burning.

That was one of the first rules he'd learned from Grampa Elie. He had also learned that just because a fire looks like it's out doesn't mean it isn't still burning down below, out of sight. Nick carefully stirred the ashes, sifting them through his fingers. Not even a little warm. That was good. Fire can get into the roots of a dry forest, keep burning out of sight, and spread. He poured water from his canteen over the ashes. A little dust rose, but no steam.

Using the sandy soil he'd placed to the side, he mixed dirt in with the ashes of his fire, then filled in more soil, followed by the pieces of sod. If he'd been near a stream, he would have poured on even more water, but filling the fire pit in this way should be fine.

He brushed off his feet, shook out his socks and slipped them on, and slid into his boots. Then, one by one, he carried each of the stones he'd placed in a semicircle back to the same exact places where he'd taken them from the hillside.

Placing his pack to one side, he brushed the moss and needles off his lean-to. He removed the branches from the sides and pulled the slipknots to untie the longer poles that formed the frame. Carefully, he distributed the sticks at random around the woods. Raking moss, leaves, and twigs over his camping area left no evidence of either a fire or a shelter. It was the way he always tried to clean up any place he'd stayed in the woods.

Leave no more sign behind than a fish does going through the water.

But this time he'd taken special care to cover where he'd been. There was no way yet that he could be absolutely sure that he was going to be followed. But the gesture Dead Eyes had made on seeing Nick survive made him sure enough.

Nick made a wide circle with his right arm, then touched his palm to his heart.

"Wliwini," he said to everything around him. "Thank you."

Which way now? he thought.

He could keep following the stream that flowed around the hill in front of him, a hill that would gradually turn into a mountain. The stream way would be easier. But more predictable.

Shouldering his pack, he began to climb the hill.

Climbing

As Nick climbed, he used a dry, straight cedar branch as a walking stick. Using the edge of his knife, he'd taken a few minutes to scrape off the branch so that it was smooth. It felt good in his hand, the way certain stones felt. Nick liked the feel of those natural things that his aunt Marge referred to as "our oldest tools."

Some of those stones you pick up, she said, *the ones that seem to fit right into your palm. Those were probably used by other people for different tasks thousands of year ago.*

Sometimes as weapons.

Nick paused and lifted his cedar walking stick. It was about five feet long, light enough to carry but heavy enough to hold up, and flexible enough to bend but not break. And strong enough to perhaps be used to defend yourself. He held the stick out, balanced it on his palm, rolled it over the back of his hand, and caught it. Then he twirled it in a figure eight, passed it behind his back from his right hand to his left, spun it overhead, and let it fall back into his right hand. He didn't go any further into the kata he'd mastered after eight years of weapons training with his pencak silat instructor. He'd done enough to have the feel of his new bo staff. Not made of Chinese whitewood, but good enough.

Hold on, dummy!

For a minute there he'd been picturing himself as one of those martial arts experts he'd seen in films, like Michelle Yeoh in *Crouching Tiger, Hidden Dragon* or Tony Jaa in *Ong Bak*. He imagined himself vanquishing hordes of attackers one by one with precise strikes and kicks. As if it would happen that way. First of all, he was still only a teenager who weighed 140 pounds. He remembered the way Dead Eyes had grabbed him on the train and manhandled him like a sack of potatoes. It showed him just how much all the self-defense he'd learned was worth when his arms were pinned and he was lifted off his feet from behind by someone bigger and stronger. And probably better trained. The way Dead Eyes held him, his forehead tight against the back of Nick's neck, showed that. There was no way that he could throw his head back against the man's nose.

The second thing was even grimmer. Was anyone pursuing him going to give him a chance to fight back hand to hand? No way! Most likely they'd just shoot him from a hundred yards away.

He shook his head and smiled. His best bet was to not be seen. To not stand out on a hillside in plain sight swinging a stick. He studied the terrain around him. A direct route to the top wouldn't be that hard. There was already a trail. It had probably been worn into the ground by generations of deer and mountain goats. He'd seen their tracks at the base and along the way in areas of soft earth as he'd climbed. Staying on the game trail would be faster. But it was exposed. And even though he'd been taking care not to leave visible footprints, there might be some signs left of his passage.

Think like a deer in hunting season.

If he veered off to the right, the slope would be stonier. There were fields of boulders and folds in the land. It would a tougher, longer climb, but his inner voice told him it was the right way to go. He'd be unseen, or at least be less visible from a distance. He continued on up the rugged slope. He stayed as low as he could, following a zigzag path. He took care not to send any loose stones rolling down the steep slopes. He went around, not over, the boulders in his way. As much as he could, he avoided any stretch where he'd be out in the open.

An hour later he was almost at the top. Twice already he'd thought he was there. Instead, he'd seen yet another slope to climb when he'd reached what was not actually the summit. The sun had crested the peak and was shining down so hard on him that he was sweating. To his right was a huge, flat rock perched on the edge of a smooth stone drop-off, like a giant slide, that went half a mile or more down the mountainside before entering the wooded slope of the forest below.

That ancient boulder, which seemed to be lodged firmly in place, had probably slid down from the mountaintop ages ago. It looked as if a sort of cave had formed beneath it. It might be a good place to get out of the sun for a little while and rest before going farther.

Nick made his way carefully over to it and rested one hand on the giant stone. Staying to one side, he carefully poked his stick into the cave. There might be animals in there, maybe even a mountain lion. He tapped the stick against the cave's floor, making a hollow sound almost like a drum beat.

Thunk-thunk, thunk-thunk.

No sound came back to indicate that anything was alive and moving about in there. Best to make doubly sure, though. Nick picked up a round stone the size of a baseball and tossed it back into the darkness. All he heard was the rattle of the rock against the cave's walls and floor. Nobody home.

"Grandfather, thank you for letting me use you as shelter," he said to the giant boulder.

Then, sliding his stick ahead of him, he knelt and crawled into the cave. It was cool and dark inside. The ceiling was high enough that he could kneel upright. Once his eyes adjusted to the darkness, he could see all around him. The cave was only about as deep as it was wide, no more than twenty feet, sloping back to the bare stone. Were those markings on the flat wall to his right? He crawled closer. Someone, taking care and showing great patience, had chiseled a shape into the gray stone. It was a man holding up his hands—perhaps in greeting or thanksgiving. Other humans before him, people native to this land, had taken shelter here before him. They'd honored this spot.

"Thank you, Old Ones," Nick said again, his voice soft.

He slid off his pack and turned to sit crosslegged facing the opening. He felt secure here. A wide vista of forest and hills beneath an impossibly blue sky stretched beyond and below as far as he could see. He had a great view. It would be impossible for anyone out there to see him when he was hidden inside the darkness of the cave.

Not that he expected to be followed already. Even if Dead Eyes or anyone helping him had come back to that train trestle, it was unlikely they would have found his trail. How would they even know whether he'd gone upstream or down? There were countless square miles of forests, hills, and mountains dotted with lakes and crossed by streams in every direction from the place he'd been tossed off the train like a bag of garbage. And there were almost no roads—aside from those used by loggers. The nearest village was on the Cree reserve where he was headed, still forty miles away.

He undid the bandanna he'd tied around his head. The fabric was strong and fast-drying. It kept sweat out of his eyes. But it was soaked. He wrung the water from it and then spread it out on the flat stone surface next to him. Then he shrugged off his jacket, planning to tie it around his waist. As he did so, the back of the coat brushed the wall of the cave, and he heard a small clinking sound. Metal striking stone.

He turned the jacket around and spread it in his lap. Something was stuck there, between the shoulders. Last night he'd thought it was a stone. But it was metal with some sort of adhesive on it. He pried it free and held it up to study it.

Crap!

He'd never seen one before, but he thought he knew what it was. A tracking device. Put there by that slap on his back before Dead Eyes had wrapped his arms around him.

That way a cleanup crew would have been able to find his dead body below the trestle to make sure he'd disappear without a trace. He hadn't died, but all the care he'd taken to cover his trail had been for nothing. With that tracker, they'd know exactly where he was.

And that was when he heard a distant thump-thump-thump. It was getting louder as it came coming closer. And now Nick knew what it was.

A helicopter.

The Sound of the Copter

escuers? Nick thought.

Maybe. But probably not. *Never break cover until you're sure.* That was another lesson Grampa Elie taught.

The sound of the helicopter was still far away. The way sound carried, it might be as far as a few miles. But the sound was getting closer. It was a good bet that someone in the copter was looking at a GPS tracker homed in on the device in Nick's hand.

If Nick stayed inside the cave, they wouldn't see him. But they'd know where he was. Maybe there would be men dropping down on lines.

Nick looked over to his left. The baseball-sized stone he'd thrown into the cave was there. He opened his pack and pulled out one of his extra pairs of wool socks and the roll of duct tape. He dropped the stone into one of the socks, wrapped it tight, and strapped the tracking device

47

onto it. Then he stuffed it into the second sock and wound more tape around it, making a solid, almost-round ball. With all that padding, Nick hoped the device would not break.

Taking careful aim and not stepping out of the mouth of the cave, Nick tossed the tape-wrapped bundle. It landed on the steepest part of the slope and started to roll. He watched as it picked up speed, bouncing now and then but not running into anything. The angle of the cave was just right so that he could see it all the way down until it disappeared half a mile below into the woods. With any luck, it would keep rolling there even longer.

The sound of the helicopter was disturbingly loud now. Right overhead. Then it suddenly was there in front of him, having come over the mountain from behind him. It was so close that Nick could see the people inside. A pilot and two other men. One of them was a man he knew all too well. Dead Eyes. But they were not looking his way.

Nick closed his own eyes, crouched down, pulled his jacket over his head, and froze. It was dark in the cave, but if they flashed a light into it, they might see him. Nothing is more recognizable faster than a human face. And there's something about looking at another person that draws their eyes to you. Even if you're going sixty miles an hour down a road, try locking eyes with a person in an oncoming car. Nine times out of ten they'll look straight back at you as they whiz by.

For several seconds, the sound of the chopper hovering in the air, no more than a few hundred feet away, was deafening. Nick could feel the wash of its blades blowing dust into the cave.

Then the sound began to lessen. It was moving away. He dared to lower the jacket and open his eyes. The helicopter was gone. He rose up to look down the mountain. The helicopter was there, so far away it seemed no larger than a dragonfly. Then it disappeared over the trees, still heading in the direction of his sock-wrapped stone and the tracking device that was in it.

Sometimes luck is even better than skill. That's what Aunt Marge used to say. And right now, if only for a brief time, luck seemed to be on his side.

Nick closed his pack, put it over his shoulder, and slid out of the cave. He had to move fast now. He scrambled up and over the top of the mountain. A maze of animal trails led down the other side. One group of trails led toward a river valley, perhaps two miles away to his left. To his right, another group of straighter trails headed to a much closer, higher valley with a smaller stream running through it. Maybe it was the one that flowed around the mountain he'd climbed to end up passing under the railroad bridge.

That straight group of trails looked easier to travel. But it was also more open to the sky, which made it easier in another way. Easier for anyone going that way to be seen from above. The trail to the left was more wooded, rockier, and rougher. It offered cover.

Nick hardly paused.

Left it is.

He began bounding down the mountain.

He'd run down slopes like this before, so he knew the difference between recklessness and speed. His legs were strong, his balance sure. His shoes provided the right amount of tread to keep from slipping and just enough stiffness to provide ankle support. He'd done some parkour training at the school where he earned his certification as a tracking teacher. That once-secret art of learning how to navigate over and around obstacles was what he needed to keep moving quickly down the steep slope. He was far from expert at it, but he'd learned how to land lightly, knees bent, and how to go into a roll and come back up running. With parkour you could almost fly over eight-foot-high walls or rough wilderness boulders.

He only paused twice to listen for the whomping of rotor blades from the sky. The first time he paused, the sound was growing more distant. The second time, the helicopter could no longer be heard. But Nick didn't slow his pace. When he reached the woods, he leapt over fallen trees and ducked under branches, avoiding open places where a footprint might be left behind. Half an hour later he saw the edge of the river through the trees.

He stopped then. Leaving the shelter of the forest without carefully scanning what was ahead would be foolish. The riverbed itself was at least fifty yards wide, but the river was only flowing in the middle of it. Nick could see berry bushes on the other side of the stream. Even from this distance, it was obvious they were laden with red fruit. Another time he would have crossed the shallow stream and lost himself picking berries. But not now.

Aside from the lazy, late-summer flow of the river, he saw nothing moving. But upstream he saw something that brought the ghost of a smile to his lips.

The Riverbank Cave

Nick slid down the pebbled bank that offered the quickest access to the river's edge. Because of that cold he'd felt coming on, he was breathing a little heavier than usual. But otherwise he felt fine. He was thirsty, but he didn't stop to drink. He was headed for what he'd seen as he scanned his surroundings—a potential hiding place a hundred feet upstream. It had been barely visible from the angle where he stood. Where the river had made a quick bend, the water seemed to have cut under a huge spruce tree that leaned over the stream. He couldn't tell how large the shadowed place he was seeing under the tree might be, but it might be deep enough.

Avoiding the sandy places, he ran lightly over the exposed bedrock bed of the river. The stream seemed to have been twice as wide as it was now, its level probably dropping soon after the spring thaw. When he reached the huge old spruce and bent to look, he saw that luck was still with him. He dropped to his knees and crawled in. He'd found yet another natural shelter. It was not a stone lean-to, like the place he'd left behind on the mountaintop, but a ten-foot-deep cave shaped from the wash of current against sand. Because the water level had dropped with summer, it wasn't the least bit moist inside. The floor was packed dry earth. Five feet overhead, it was roofed with living roots, and light filtered in through a space between two of the widest ones.

Nick crawled to the back of the small cave and took a deep breath. He leaned against the mat of thin, feathery roots that covered the back wall. They gave just enough with his weight to feel like a hammock.

His heart was pounding, but he wasn't exhausted. He hadn't burned himself out the way someone might who was running on adrenaline. He could have kept running, putting more distance between him and the men in the copter. But that might just be what they expected. Doing the unexpected was one way to keep from being caught. Fleeing in blind panic and getting caught out in the open was the worst thing someone could do when being pursued from above.

His mind was racing, though. Where were his pursuers now? What should he do next? Would he ever see his parents again?

Too many thoughts were crowding his head. He needed to calm himself down.

He closed his eyes and started doing the breathing exercise he'd begun to learn when he was ten. Black Tiger Breathing. He hadn't been shown it by any teacher. He'd found it in a book about Northern Chinese styles of kung fu.

All you had to do was sit quietly and inhale. And keep inhaling in one single extended breath for at least thirty seconds. Then you had to settle that breath down low into your center of chi, your diaphragm area, and hold it there for twenty seconds. Finally, you had to release that breath, once again slowly in a single exhalation, for another thirty seconds.

The book said it was a way to build your chi, that internal strength the old masters of martial arts called the center of everything and nothing. Focus on breathing and counting. Put everything else out of your mind.

From the description in the book, it had seemed like something easy to do. But it wasn't. The first time Nick had tried it, he found himself gasping for breath after trying to just breathe in for a count of eight. But he had always been determined, even when he was much younger.

His parents still told the story of what happened when Nick was four years old and they gave him a simple toy. It was a wooden ball attached by a string to a little wooden cup with a handle on it. The objective was to hold the handle and then swing the ball up and catch it in the cup that was just big enough for it to fit into. It was an Abenaki game that—like most of the old things Native kids played with—wasn't just for fun. In this case its purpose was to build eye–hand coordination. It looked simple, but catching that ball in the cup was difficult. The first ten times Nick tried, the ball either bounced off the cup or missed it entirely. That's when most four-year-olds would have quit.

"But not our Nick," his mother would tell people. "This look came over his little face and he kept trying. Even when he finally caught the ball, he didn't quit. He kept going, time after time, just about the whole morning. He did not stop until he was able to do it ten times in a row."

And that was the way Nick approached Black Tiger Breathing when he was ten years old. By the end of a week, he could draw the air into his lungs for that count of eight. However, holding that breath and then releasing it just as slowly was even more difficult. He continued trying, though. By the end of a month, he was up to an even count of twenty on each end—out and in—with ten in the middle.

But that was when he realized he was hurrying his count. So he tried slowing that down by counting not one, two, three, but one and one thousand, two and one thousand, three and one thousand, and so on.

It was not until he reached a full count of thirty in, twenty held, thirty out that he decided to look at his watch as he did it. And that had made him smile. Because each cycle of thirty-twenty-thirty was taking him exactly one minute and twenty seconds.

Inside his riverbank cave, Nick breathed. All he thought of was counting and breathing. Counting and breathing.

In, hold, out. In, hold, out. In, hold, out.

He felt his body relaxing. A calm he'd not felt since he had taken that wrong turn in the train corridor settled over him.

And, as he finished his breathing exercise, he realized that his head had cleared. His ears and his sinuses no longer felt stuffed up. However, as soon as they cleared, he realized two things that made his heart beat faster.

The first was that he could hear the thud-thud-thud of a helicopter coming closer. The second was that he could smell something he'd not been able to notice before with a congested nose. It wasn't an unpleasant smell, but it was one he recognized. The scent of a bear. The little riverbank cave he'd crawled into was one of its denning places.

CHAPTER

11

The Roar

The thudding sound of the helicopter was so close now that Nick could feel it as much as hear it. Had they figured out some other way to find him? Despite the care he took, had he left any signs as he ran? Did they know where he was now?

Or were they just searching every possible place he might have gone? After diving down into the valley to follow the beacon he'd taped to that rock, maybe they'd tried circling the mountain. And after not finding him, did they go up and down the different valleys to the east of the high place where he'd been? That might be more likely. So far, it seemed as if there was only the one helicopter. When Nick caught sight of it, he'd noticed that it wasn't a really big one. It looked like an old military copter, maybe an Apache, painted camouflage green. It could not hold many passengers. That meant there couldn't

be that many people looking for him now—Dead
Eyes, the pilot, and one or two others.

The sound of the copter's blade was not quite
as loud now. It meant they weren't hovering
directly overhead. He edged forward in the cave,
just far enough to see out the opening but still
far enough back that he would not be visible
from the outside. The helicopter was flying low
a hundred yards downriver from him. So low
the wind from its rotors was stripping leaves
from the riverside alders and flattening the brush
under it. An Apache, for sure, but not a new
one. And it seemed to have been stripped of its
weapons. No Hellfire tank-killer missiles on its
lower sides, and no big chain gun sticking out
the front. Probably stripped before being sold for
civilian use.

But still deadly. Nick could see the figure of a
man leaning halfway out the door with a rifle in
his hands. The copter turned, and he could make
out enough of the man's upper body to see that he
was lanky and had bushy yellow hair worn like
an Afro. He wasn't bald and muscled like a weight
lifter, like Dead Eyes. A strap was fastened to the
back of the harness that Blondie wore. He could
lean far out, with his hands free to handle his
weapon, without being in danger of falling. From
the easy way Blondie was positioning himself, it

looked as if he'd done this sort of thing before. Maybe he was one of those guys Nick despised, the ones who used to shoot wolves in Alaska from helicopters. Except now he was hunting even bigger game.

Blondie waved one hand, pointing down, and the Apache turned again, heading back downriver. Toward his hiding place. Nick bit his lower lip. But the helicopter suddenly veered away from Nick's side, swooping toward the thick tangle of berry bushes across the stream from him.

Something was moving over there. Nick couldn't see the thing itself, but he saw the way the brush was being moved as it thrashed one way and the next as the copter came closer. Blondie was leaning farther out, pointing the rifle down. Suddenly, Nick heard the crack of the rifle and saw the burst of flame from its barrel as the blond-haired man fired, answered by a roar. It was so loud that it could be heard even over the deafening sounds of the Apache's four blades and powerful engine.

Then the thing that let out that roar stood up from the cover of the berry bushes. A huge brown bear. Blondie was not firing again. It wasn't what they were after. A hand was on his shoulder, pulling him back into the helicopter. Nick saw that as the helicopter rose higher and passed over him, heading back toward the mountain.

But he only saw it out of the corner of his eye. What he was truly focused on was in front of him. The bear. It had dropped back to all fours and started to run. Pebbles and sand were thrown up by its feet as it charged down the riverbank, then splashed into the stream. Nick could hear it breathing hard as it ran.

Chuff! Chuff! Chuff! Chuff!

It was heading for the nearest place of refuge it knew. Heading straight toward him. Straight toward its riverbank den under the old spruce tree.

Bear Song

It was happening fast. Too fast for Nick to move. But not too fast for him to think. Even if he had the time to dive for the opening of the cave, he'd run headfirst into the bear. And even if the bear didn't maul him—or worse—he would be out in the open, visible to the men in the helicopter who might still be watching.

What came to his mind then was something his grandfather had shared with him one spring day when Nick was twelve years old. They'd found the tracks of a black bear as they walked an Adirondack Mountain trail leading up toward Algonquin Peak. His grandfather had dropped to one knee and pulled up his pants leg to show Nick the tattoo he had there. The tattoo of a bear paw. Its shape was exactly like that of the print his grandfather pointed out to him in the moist sand where a small stream washed over the edge of the trail.

"Bear's our older brother," his grandfather had said. Then he'd sung Nick the "Bear Path Song."

> Dabi nawan ginose ya ni neh
> Dabi nawan ginose ya ni neh
> Mukawdewakumig
> Mukawdewakumig

Nick knelt back down. He bent his head, crossing his arms in front of his face. He could hear his grandfather's voice singing that song about walking a calm and peaceful way upon the earth. He could actually hear the song itself. Then he realized that what he heard was his own voice singing it.

The whole cave shook as the huge grizzly shouldered its way in. Its body blocked out the light and everything became dark.

HRRRMMMPPPHHH, the bear growled. It had caught the sight and scent of him.

Nick didn't look up. He kept giving his voice to the old, old song. Half of his mind was on the song. The other half was saying a silent apology to the bear.

Grandfather, take pity on me. Forgive me for intruding into your place.

> Dabi nawan ginose ya ni neh
> Dabi nawan ginose ya ni neh

Mukawdewakumig

Mukawdewakumig

The bear was growling softly. Nick could feel the warm, wet heat of its body. He could feel it looking at him. He didn't look up. He kept singing. He felt it come closer. Its breath was washing over him. Any second he might feel its claws slashing across him, its jaws tearing at his flesh. He pushed that thought away, pushed away the fear. There was nothing he could do except to sing and ask for the bear to forgive him.

Grandfather, Grandfather, take pity, take pity on me.

One of the bear's huge front paws thrust forward, but not in a raking blow that would have torn him apart. The bear's foot was placed flat onto his chest, pushing him against the matted roots at the back of the den. Then the bear's square head nudged his hands aside, and Nick saw it open its enormous mouth—so big it could crush his head with one bite. He could smell the berries it had been eating on its breath. It bit down on his left shoulder, hard enough that its teeth bruised his flesh, but not hard enough to make him bleed or break bones. The bear growled again, a deeper growl that Nick could feel all through his body as it lifted him up a few inches. The bear moved its head back and forth a little, gently shaking him. Somehow, Nick didn't feel any pain.

He kept singing.

Dabi nawan ginose ya ni neh
Dabi nawan ginose ya ni neh
Mukawdewakumig
Mukawdewakumig

The bear opened its mouth, letting Nick slide back down into a sitting position. It drew back its paw from his chest. Then, with a heavy motion that again made the whole den shake, the grizzly turned and dropped its huge body in front of him, its head toward the mouth of the cave.

Nick did not stop singing. He could hear the sound of the bear's breathing, almost in rhythm with the "Bear Path Song." The big grizzly's even, strong breath and his own song were all he could hear at first. Then he heard a voice, a deep rough voice, a voice without breath that spoke inside his head.

Rest, Grandson, it growled.

And then he heard nothing as his eyes closed and he fell into a dream.

He was walking through a calm forest of tall evergreens. His right hand was resting on the back of the grizzly as it walked beside him. And this time it was the grizzly who was singing the "Bear Path Song" as they traveled together. Everything around them was peaceful.

Going Slow

ick opened his eyes. The bear was gone. He felt his shoulder where the bear had grabbed him. It ached a little, but he didn't seem to be badly hurt. He slid toward the entrance and looked out. It was night, the moonlight flickering on the moving waters of the stream. He looked at the glowing dial of his watch. It read four o'clock.

Four a.m. He'd slept most of the night. The sun would be rising soon. What should he do now?

Think. Think about what had happened so far and what that meant about what he should do next.

Clearly, the murder he'd seen on the train was something important. If it wasn't, they wouldn't be after him with a helicopter. Maybe that murdered person, the man who looked sort of Asian, was the key. Nick had seen both him and Dead Eyes. He'd never forget either of their faces. So now Nick had to be eliminated. The people after him were not going to give up easily. He had to keep running.

Getting to that nearest First Nations reserve was still a good idea. There would be a tribal police station. Once he was with law enforcement people and he'd told his story, he would probably be safe.

He was surely still being chased. The fact that they'd pursued him from the air showed how determined they were to get him. And if they used a copter once, they could do it again. He'd read up online about this part of the province. If what he remembered was right, the area between him and the reserve hadn't been logged in years. The forest ahead was thick. He could try to keep under the cover of the trees. But there'd be places where he would still be visible from the air.

And they might put other men on the ground, maybe specialists who'd been trained as man hunters. Like guys who'd had Special Forces or Rangers training. They'd start from the hilltop where they'd first picked up the beacon he'd thrown away.

They'll expect me to be scared, to run and keep running, Nick thought. And when you run that way, you always leave a trail. Which meant he had to be deliberate. Keep toward his goal, but do it more slowly now.

He thought about another lesson he'd learned when it came to tracking. A really good tracker doesn't need tracks to follow. His teacher had told him about Uncle Jimmy Johnson, who was the greatest Aboriginal tracker in Australia. When Uncle Jimmy was sent out to find someone, a hiker who got lost or a fugitive, all he needed to see was where their tracks began. Then he could figure out where that person was going to end up. And he would go to that place, take a seat on a rock, and wait for them to appear.

Someone good at tracking might do just that to him. Dope out where he was headed, and be there waiting for him just before he got there. But maybe not. From what Nick had seen of Blondie, the guy with the rifle who shot at the bear, he didn't seem like the expert tracker type. And Dead Eyes? Again, Nick had a gut feeling that he was not a real tracker either. A killer, but not someone who knows the woods and has, as Grampa Elie put it, shaken hands with the land. And the copter pilot was probably just that—a man most comfortable when he was at the controls of a flying machine.

No, they all seemed more the type to first hunt from above—with that copter. And then, when on the ground, to not move the way Nick was taught. Their feet would be heavy on the earth.

So, Nick thought, *the best tactic right now may be to stay put after all. Stay right here because, thanks to that bear, this is the one place they'll never expect me to be.*

He looked again at his watch. It was now 4:15. About two hours till sunrise. Time for breakfast. He slid out of the cave and waded into the river. There was just enough light from the moon for him to see the pool ahead of him that had a large, flat rock at the bottom, perhaps four feet below the surface. He moved toward it slowly, deliberately.

Nick had learned all kinds of ways to fish, including how to make a line by reverse wrapping the fibers of plants, how to make a hook from a piece of bone, and how to build a fish trap by creating a weir that could direct the fish into it. But right now he had a more direct, faster method in mind.

When the bear came splashing across the stream, Nick had seen a flash of motion in the water. A ripple of light underwater heading toward that flat stone. He was almost at the stone now. He bent his knees and ducked his head underwater, his hands grasping the stone. Then, moving a finger's width at a time, first one hand and then the other slid under the stone. He couldn't see, but he didn't need to see. He based everything on feeling now. The fingers of one hand and then the other caressed the smooth, trembling side of the fish. He began to stroke it, cupping it between his palms.

Thank you for giving yourself to me, Nick thought as his caress turned into a firm grasp and he pulled the trout, which was as long and thick as his forearm, out from its hiding place. He carried it back to the bank.

"May you continue to swim," he said, speaking the words thousands of generations of his ancestors had spoken before him. Then, holding the unresisting fish firm on the ground with his left hand, he struck it on the back of its neck with a rock held in his right hand, releasing its spirit back into the water with one quick blow.

Ferns

A full day had now passed since the big trout gave itself to him. Nick had seen no sign of the copter. It seemed as if their search for him had moved on.

But it had not stopped. He felt certain of that. The men who wanted him dead were still out there, somewhere ahead of him. He'd moved out of the bear's den by the river.

"Wliwini, ktsi awasos," he'd said, raising his hand toward the berry bushes where he did not doubt the bear was waiting to reclaim its resting place. "Thank you, great bear."

Then he'd found another shelter under the wide-spreading roots of a big, blown-down cedar. He'd eaten, rested, taken more time to think.

Know your enemy. Nick couldn't remember where he'd first heard that or if it was something he'd read. Was it *The Book of Five Rings* by Musashi Miyamoto, the greatest of all the Japanese samurai warriors? Or maybe *The Art of War* by Sun Tzu, the famous fourth-century BC Chinese general? Maybe both. What he knew for sure was that it was true. That kind of knowing meant knowing more if your enemy didn't know you. It also meant knowing yourself. What you were capable of, what you could do.

Nick smiled as a story he did remember for sure surfaced in his mind. It was called "The Most Dangerous Game" and was the tale of a man named Rainsford who found himself stranded on an island where he was released into the jungle by a Russian general who'd gotten bored with hunting wild animals and now was hunting humans because they were the most dangerous game of all. It had been one of Grampa Elie's favorite stories.

Nick shook his head.

I'm not going to fool myself, Nick thought. Malay man-catchers, Burmese tiger pits, Ugandan knife traps all sounded like great ideas in that story. But in real life, would those work? Especially when you're not on an island but have millions of acres ahead of you?

Then he smiled again. Even though those ideas might not be really practical, he could still turn things around by staying a step or two ahead. One of Grampa Elie's friends who was in the Marines with him in Vietnam was a Cheyenne man named Lance.

"My friend Lance told me," Grampa Elie said, "the only time the Army ever caught up with his people was when they were not trying to get away from anyone. Those awful massacres of Cheyennes at the Washita and Sand Creek happened because those were peaceful villages, out in plain sight and flying an American flag in front of their chief's lodge. But when General Custer and all of them went after Cheyennes who were at war, the white soldiers just never caught up with them. That was because those Cheyennes made sure not to be anywhere they were expected to be."

And that, Nick thought, *is where I have to be. Where I'm not expected.*

He shouldered his pack. The sun had not yet risen, but there was plenty of light from the moonlit sky. He'd charted a course for himself using the map. By taking note of the elevations and the rivers and streams, he was pretty sure he'd be able to avoid the areas where things could get rough—swamps, or gorges where you'd have to climb down and then up the other side. Places he might get stuck or find himself caught out in the open.

But he was not going to take the easiest routes toward the reserve. Not the most direct routes like the old logging tracks or the snowmobile and hiking trails marked on the map. Those were the places where he'd be expected, where someone might be waiting in ambush.

Nick brushed his palm over the sword ferns that were growing around him in abundance. He'd read wild-plant guides for the region and also learned from some of the Salish elders he had met. There was food all around you if you knew where and when to look. In the spring, sword ferns were good eating. When they were just rising out of the ground, coiled up like fiddleheads. And their tubers down in the moist earth were good to eat.

Ferns had lessons to teach too. Aunt Marge had pointed out some of those lessons to him when he was really young. She'd been working on making an elm bark basket. With a sharp stick she was making patterns on the outside of the basket. Curled patterns like ferns that were uncoiling.

"See this," she had said. "It's a story about hunting and tracking."

Then she'd explained that when a deer is being chased, that deer does not just run straight to get away. It circles and maybe goes up onto a rise so it can look back over its own tracks and see whoever or whatever is after it. Its path is like that of a curving young fern. A good hunter knows that and makes another circle to come up behind the animal that's being tracked.

What I need to do now, Nick thought, *is be both the deer and the hunter.*

Ahead of him was one of the hiking trails he'd found on his map. He shifted his walking stick into his left hand and began to run. For the next three hours, before the sunrise filled the sky ahead of him, Nick followed the trail east. He loped along at an easy pace. But when the sun was about to crest the mountains, with birds starting to sing all around him, he stopped.

He turned and ducked under the thick bunches of old-man's-beard lichen hanging down from the branches of the trees along the trail. He made his way through thick ferns, brushing them aside and taking care not to crush any underfoot. Twenty yards ahead, a huge hemlock tree had fallen halfway up the slope south of the trail. When he reached the tree, he put both hands on it, then vaulted lightly up onto its wide, mossy top.

He paused there. Nick had learned—when he was seven years old—to always look before you leap when you're out in nature. It happened in New Mexico. His Aunt Marge had grabbed him by the arm and stopped him halfway through stepping over a big rock. He'd almost landed on a western diamondback rattler sunning itself.

There wasn't much chance of running into a poisonous snake here. He'd be more likely to land on a banana slug or a salamander. But he didn't want to do that. It wasn't right for anything to be hurt because of his carelessness. He studied the ground. Nothing there. He dropped down, landing in a crouch and not straightening up.

He stayed there, unmoving, breathing slowly and listening. A soft chirp came from someplace next to him. He turned his head slightly to his left and saw a tree frog. It chirruped again, its red eyes peering out at him from the crevice in the old tree's bark that was its home. Nick nodded to it and continued to listen. A ray of sunlight sifted through the branches laden with moss and lichen. As the beam of light touched the trail below him, it was as if a switch had been thrown. The chorus of birds began. Thrushes and warblers and sparrows and other birds he couldn't name raised their voices, the forest echoing with their songs.

Nick was no stranger to that greeting of the new day. He couldn't count all the times he'd woken in one woodland or another to hear the dawn chorus of the winged ones. It moved him now as it always did. There were men somewhere ahead who wanted to kill him. But there was still so much in nature to bring a smile to his face, to put sunshine in his heart.

"Wliwini, wli dogo wongan," he whispered. "Thank you, all my relations."

It wasn't just the beauty of their songs that made Nick feel good. It was what that singing meant, singing that went on unbroken minute after minute. If there were other people around, people who didn't know enough to be still and just listen, that singing would have stopped. A silent forest is a forest where predators are moving about. He could relax.

Nick leaned back against a dry spot on the side of the fallen hemlock. He opened his pack and took out a piece of maple-cured jerky. He tore off a small piece and placed it on the ground.

"I share my food with all you little ones," he said in a low, soft voice, speaking the way Grampa Elie had taught him to speak in the forest. It showed respect and also did not carry the way more careless human voices did.

He bit off a piece of the jerky. He ate it slowly, washing it down with sips of water from his canteen. He concentrated on how satisfying the water felt as he drank it, how good the jerky tasted as he chewed each bite. How comfortable it was sitting on the soft earth, leaning back on the fallen hemlock, feeling a soft morning breeze on his face, smelling the air, and listening to the birds. He didn't think about what he had to do next or what might happen later in the day— good or bad. "Sometimes," Grampa Elie would say, "you just need to be. Not a human doing, but a human being. Then, when it is time to do, you'll usually do it a whole lot better."

Nick closed his eyes and slipped into Black Tiger Breathing. In, hold, out again. Twenty times. By the time he was done, the sun was fully up. The forest around him was not silent, but that overwhelming chorus of all birds had ended.

Time to be the hunter, he thought. He took out his map and compass.

They Don't Know Me

ick's plan was simple. Don't stay on the trails but stay in sight of the trails, whether old logging roads, snowmobile tracks, or hiking paths. Keep circling up to places higher than those ways leading toward the reserve. Never get closer to the trail than fifty yards away. Move quickly when you move. Don't stomp down heel first like someone unused to forest paths would walk. Roll your foot so that even when you step on a twig it doesn't make a loud crack. Keep moving that way, just short of a trot. Then stop and wait. Listen and look before starting to move again.

This was not a part of the province where many people went at this time of year. That was clear all through the day after Nick left his shelter under the wide roots of the blown-down cedar. He saw no sign of any humans—either the men hunting him or innocent hikers. But he didn't allow himself to become careless.

Move, then stop and listen. Move, then stop and listen. There were always sounds to be heard when he did that. Once it was a whole family of raccoons, six babies following their mother, growling and wrestling with each other as they trundled along. Another time it was a deer, and yet another time a solitary wolf that only recognized a human was nearby after it had gone past him. Then, having caught Nick's scent on the wind, it leapt off the trail to go zigzagging through the forest until it was out of sight. And often, more than a dozen times, what Nick heard when he made one of those silent waits were the sounds of squirrels, making more noise than bears as they rustled along the forest floor.

He'd picked up a piece of red cedar as he'd walked. It was a branch as long as the distance from the fingers of his outstretched hand to his elbow. Heavy and half the thickness of his wrist, it was the perfect size for a rabbit stick. Each time he stopped, he took out his knife and scraped it down the length of the stick, smoothing it and making it better fit his grasp.

Nick had always been unusually good at throwing. The coaches in grade school and middle school had tried to recruit him for Little League Baseball after seeing how far, hard, and accurately he could send a baseball with almost no effort.

But Nick had preferred to spend his time on other things—reading, outdoor skills, and martial arts, especially after he started spending summers in New Mexico at The Tracking Project.

The first time he'd been shown how a rabbit stick was used to hunt small game in Australia, Africa, and among North American Native people, he'd fallen in love with it. Soon he could hit targets a hundred feet away with the traditional sidearm throw that sent the stick spinning. And it worked for things other than rabbits. When one of The Tracking Project students had been chased by a mugger in Central Park, she had grabbed a stick off the ground as she ran, turned, threw it, and knocked the guy out!

Nick hefted the rabbit stick. It made him feel as if he was in contact with thousands of generations of people who'd used this ancient way to hunt—or defend themselves. Simple, easy, effective. An old movie came to mind, one that was supposed to be about an actual tracker but had gotten corny real fast. Tommy Lee Jones played the tracker, who was hunting and being hunted by his best former student. In the final scene, the two of them make weapons to fight each other. One of them makes a hunting knife out of flint while the other builds a portable blast furnace to forge a steel weapon. As if they had the time to do that! Thinking of it made Nick smile at how silly it was.

He stopped and slowly crouched down. Had he heard something? The forest here on this ridge above the trail was thick, but maybe not thick enough for someone looking down from the air. Nick slid under the low, thick branches of a hemlock. Now he could hear the sound of a helicopter's thudding blades. He fought the urge to look up as the copter swept overhead . . . and kept going. He hadn't been seen.

Nick waited until he was certain it was gone. Then he took out the map. The trees were too closely grown here for a helicopter to touch down. But the map showed an area five miles farther ahead where several of the trails came together. A small settlement had once been there. A logging town. There'd be places there where it could land. And it was between Nick and the reserve.

That was it. Nick felt he knew what Dead Eyes had in mind. They'd be waiting there for him to show up, since all the trails led that way. They'd be hiding, and he would be easy prey, worn out from running, tired, hungry, and desperate. That's how they thought he'd be, how most people would be in his situation.

But they don't know me, Nick thought. *They don't know me.*

The Copter

It was almost dark when Nick reached the place where the trails came together at the ghost town. But he'd followed none of those trails. He'd gone around. He'd made a mile-wide circle so that he first caught sight of the deserted logging town from a hill to the east, not the west. What told him he'd been right in being so careful was down there. The Apache helicopter. It sat on the far eastern end of the abandoned settlement on a wide area behind what might once have been a one-room school. Though grass was growing up between cracks in the paved yard, the concrete breaking down to sand, it was a clear enough surface for a makeshift landing pad.

No one seemed to be guarding it. But Nick stayed where he was, a quarter of a mile away on a wooded hill looking down on the ghost town. The trees and brush were thick there, and he could watch through the green screen of leaves and branches without being seen. He watched and waited until he saw the glow of light through the windows of one of the buildings.

City people, he thought. *They have to have light, even when they don't need it. Even on a night when the moon is so bright it casts a shadow.*

That light in the building was a good sign. It meant the men trying to catch him were not real trackers, people comfortable with being in a forest. They needed light to feel secure. It also meant they weren't worried about anything being a threat to them. But real hunters realize no one is ever fully in control of nature. You always have to be alert.

How dangerous could one skinny kid be? they were probably thinking.

Nick smiled, a thin, tight smile that didn't show his teeth. *Dangerous enough*, he thought. He tapped the rabbit stick in the palm of his left hand.

The full moon was now four hands high in the southern sky. Nick made his way down the hill, paused, and listened. Then, staying in the shadows, he moved on to the helicopter. The pilot's side was open. No door. The moon over his shoulder shone into the cockpit. He climbed in and sat in the pilot's seat. Nick had read about helicopters and how to fly them.

He recognized the three main controls. Foot pedals to control the rotor blades and rotate the copter. A collective lever on his left side to angle the rotor blades. Pull it back to go up, and push it forward to go down. Then there was the cyclic, the big joystick between his legs. You could use it to make the machine go forward or backward, left or right.

But knowing all that was far different from actually flying a whirlybird. No way was he going to even try.

He took his knife out of its sheath. *I could cut some of the wires and cables*, he thought. Then he shook his head. *Better to not let them know I was here.*

He put his knife away. He knew a better way to disable a helicopter.

When started to get up from the pilot's seat, he saw something behind the passenger seat. Two things. The first was under a blanket with just an edge of it visible. It was leather with beadwork. Nick moved the blanket, uncovering the briefcase he'd seen in the murdered man's stateroom.

You're coming with me, he thought. Nick pulled out the briefcase, tucking the blanket back so that it looked as if nothing had been disturbed.

Then he slid out the second thing he'd seen. The rifle that had been placed under the back seat.

It was a .308, just like the one Grampa Elie owned. It was fully loaded and almost certainly the gun that Blondie had used when he was shooting at the bear near the river.

Now's the time, Nick thought, *when in a movie I'd be going all Rambo. Charge the building and mow everyone down.*

He shook his head. It wasn't that he didn't know how to use the gun. Killing people, even men wanting to take his life? That just wasn't him. But there was something else he could do. He'd learned how to take apart a rifle just like this to clean it. Maybe he couldn't do it blindfolded—like his grandfather—but what he could do would not take that long. He took out the magazine, cleared the breech, popped out the take-down pins with his fingers, and pulled the charging handle back. The bolt came out. With the tip of his knife, he pulled out the retaining pin, and the firing pin dropped free.

No firing pin, no shoot.

Nick dropped the firing pin into his shirt pocket, reassembled the rifle, and placed it back where it had been. He slid out of the helicopter and stood listening for a time without moving. Nothing.

And now it's time to ground this bird, he thought.

He reached up and unscrewed the cap on the top of the Apache's fuel tank below the main rotor. A discarded fast-food coffee cup had been tossed onto the ground. He scooped it full of sand and dumped the sand into the fuel tank. He did that once, twice, three times before placing the cup back where it had been on the ground. He picked up the fuel cap and screwed it on tight.

Enjoy walking, gentlemen, he thought.

Then, with the briefcase tucked under his arm, he climbed back up to his vantage point on the hill.

Curiosity

Curiosity killed the cat. That was one of Grampa Elie's sayings.

Perhaps Nick should have just headed straight toward the reserve. By his map it was only fifteen miles away now, and the unmaintained road between the reserve and the abandoned logging town looked to be a straight shot. But Nick was curious about two things. The first was what would happen when they tried to start that helicopter. Wanting to know that did make sense. If, despite the sand in the gas, it could fly, then they'd still be able to search for him from above.

The other thing he was curious about was the briefcase. It was heavy, stuffed with something. Clearly something important to Dead Eyes or he would not have taken it with him. Money? Bearer bonds? Whatever it was, it had been worth a man's life.

There was enough dawn light now for Nick to see clearly to read. And from his place concealed on the hill, he could still keep an eye on the copter and see anyone who might be coming his way—though he doubted the men hunting him had realized he was there.

He opened the briefcase. No money, just documents and a thick plastic bag with thumb drives in it.

It didn't take long for him to figure out who the murdered man had been. A lawyer. His name was Nathaniel Ho, and his offices were in Ottawa. That was what it said on his business cards, as well as on the driver's license and credit cards inside the wallet Nick found shoved down into the bottom of the briefcase.

Why he'd been killed took Nick a little more time to figure out. But when he saw the names—circled in yellow with a highlighter—in one of the documents, he began to understand. The document was the transcript of a secretly recorded conversation—probably on one of those thumb drives. The names were of two very important men in the Canadian government. The conversation was about payoffs for clearing the way to set up oil-fracking operations on First Nations lands. The oil exploration the other Natives on the train had been talking about. Those lands included the reserve where Nick was heading. The lawyer had been employed by a group of First Nations tribes to help stop the drilling. And he'd been doing his job too well. A chill went down Nick's back. This was way bigger than he'd suspected.

Nick closed the briefcase. Taking a length of string cord, he fastened it to the back of his pack.

Think. What does this mean?

Were Dead Eyes and Blondie and the copter pilot the only ones after him? Or were others being called in? Would others be waiting for him at the reserve? *Be logical.*

Trust your intuition. That's what Aunt Marge said. And his intuition was telling him that there would not be more pursuers. Dead Eyes had screwed up by not just having a witness but by also letting him get away. The fewer who knew, the better. The more people involved, the more likely the killer's mistake would be known and he'd be in big trouble.

What Nick had to do now was make sure that more people knew about what had happened— about the killing, and about what was in the briefcase. Safety in numbers.

Reach the reserve. Find the office of the tribal police.

There was movement below. Three men were walking toward the copter.

CHAPTER

Found

It was Dead Eyes, Blondie, and a tall, skinny man Nick assumed was the pilot. The three of them moved with calm assurance to the copter.

Sure of themselves, Nick thought.

The pilot climbed in on his side, and the other two followed him. Dead Eyes settled into the front seat, while Blondie climbed in back, pulled out his rifle, and cradled it in his arms. Nick watched as they strapped in and the pilot leaned forward to start the engine. It started to turn over, but the clanking, grinding sounds that followed were pleasing to only one set of ears—Nick's. The helicopter's blades turned once, then the whole machine shook. It didn't blow up—like in a Hollywood film—but the cloud of black smoke that shot out of the machine's exhaust pipe and was carried away by the wind was satisfying enough.

The three men climbed out of the disabled helicopter. Dead Eyes was holding the blanket that had been covering the briefcase. The wind was too strong now for Nick to hear what they were saying, but from the way Dead Eyes was waving his arms, it was not a happy conversation. The bald assassin's degree of displeasure was made even more clear when he knocked the pilot down and began to kick him.

But Dead Eyes only kicked him twice before stopping, turning, and staring up at the hill where Nick was watching.

It sent a shiver down Nick's spine. Even though he was certain there was no way he could be seen, concealed as he was, far away as he was, he still closed his eyes.

When he opened them again, Dead Eyes was no longer looking his way. He had something in his hand and seemed to be talking into it. It looked like a satellite phone or a walkie-talkie. The pilot was still on the ground, curled into a defensive ball. Blondie was running back toward the building where they'd spent the night.

Crap, Nick thought. There might be no way he could have been seen, but somehow—he knew in his gut—Dead Eyes had sensed him. He had to move fast. He slid down the other side of the hill to the trail below it and began to run.

As he ran, he was thinking ahead, making sense of what he'd just observed. The helicopter was out of the equation now. But Dead Eyes had been communicating with someone. Maybe someone who was waiting on the reserve. That was one thing. The other was the way Blondie was hurrying back to the old town as if to get something. Nick hoped it wasn't what he thought it might be.

He'd covered at least a mile now. It was hilly, one hill after another, but easy running. The trail he was on had once been a road. Back when the logging town was in its heyday, there'd been trucks on that road. And the town had electricity then. There were still utility poles, short ones, along the old road. The remnants of broken wires that once carried phone messages and power drooped like vines from some of them.

"They say there's five senses," Grampa Elie had said to him. "Seeing, hearing, touching, tasting, and smelling. But there's also the one I call feeling, when you feel something beyond what those five other senses tell you, and you just know it's true."

That feeling sense was now telling Nick what to do as he kept running, even though he hadn't yet heard the sound that would tell him what he felt was right. He stayed on the old logging road as it rose up over another rise, then curved right on the other side to bypass a deep gully and go between two straight, good-sized trees. Nick stopped. A thin electric wire hung down from where it had been fastened onto one of those straight trees.

Nick stuck his rabbit stick under his belt. He grabbed the wire and pulled on it. He stumbled back as a twenty-foot length of cable came free. He looped one end around the tree that had held the wire, chest high, then wrapped it around itself to fasten it tight. Next, he looped the other end of wire around the other tree, pulling it taut and tying it just as firmly. The way the road dipped and curved there, that dark wire across it wouldn't be visible right away to anyone coming fast down the trail. A runner would see it, but not . . .

RRRRRRMMMMM!

The sudden sound from the road behind him told Nick his intuition had been correct. Three hills back, they came into sight. Dead Eyes and Blondie on a four-wheel ATV, going at least forty miles an hour. Dead Eyes was driving. Blondie, rifle slung over his shoulder, was on the back.

They'd seen him. Nick turned, pausing to make sure they saw the briefcase tied to his pack, just before they went down the hill and he was out of sight. Then he began to run.

Keep your eyes on me, he thought, not looking back, but counting as he ran, the roar of the ATV getting louder, closer.

One, two, three, four . . . WHAM!

At the sound of the crash, he stopped to look back. The ATV was on its side, no longer running, but its wheels were still spinning. Blondie was pinned under it and not moving. Nick began to walk back toward it. Those men might have been trying to kill him, but he couldn't just leave if they were badly injured and he could help them.

As he came closer, now less than a hundred feet away, Nick still didn't see Dead Eyes. Had the wire across the road taken him out too?

Nick stopped when he saw motion off to the right. A man was pulling himself stiffly up the slope from where he'd been thrown into the gully. Dead Eyes. He bent over and picked up the rifle that had been slung over Blondie's back. Then he turned, glared in Nick's direction, and raised the rifle to his shoulder. Dead Eyes showed his teeth in a wolfish smile, blood dripping from the corner of his mouth. At this range—fifty feet away now—he couldn't miss. Nick didn't move. It was quiet now. The wheels of the ATV were no longer spinning

This is the point, Nick thought, *when bad guys in books and movies make little speeches about why*

they are doing whatever it is they're doing and what they're going to do to the good guy.

But instead of making a speech, Dead Eyes just pulled the trigger. Nothing happened aside from a clicking sound. He looked at the rifle, ejected the unspent round, and jacked a new bullet into the chamber. He aimed a second time at Nick—who was now standing with his hands out to the side, palms up. Once again he pulled the trigger. And the gun didn't fire.

Nick reached into his pocket, pulled out the firing pin, and held it up.

Dead Eyes growled, dropped the rifle, and charged head-down at Nick.

Again, Nick didn't move. At least not until the last second. That was when he stepped to the side and hit Dead Eyes in the back of his head with the rabbit stick. The burly man went down like a puppet with its strings cut.

He was still breathing. So was Blondie, even though it looked as if he had a broken ankle after Nick pried the ATV back upright. It didn't take long for Nick to strap the two men's arms together behind their backs, elbows first, then wrists, making the bonds more secure with a layer of electric wire. Ankles next. Then, after dragging each of them to separate trees and sitting them up,

Nick used the rest of the roll of duct tape from his bag to fasten them in place.

A crackling sound was coming from down the slope where Dead Eyes had been thrown. It was a two-way radio. As Nick picked it up, a voice came out of the walkie-talkie.

"Alpha One, this is Bravo. Have you secured the package?'

Nick thought for a moment, then pressed the SEND key. "Bravo," he said, lowering his voice into a growl that he hoped sounded like Dead Eyes, "Abort! Abort!"

He pulled the back off the radio, popped out the batteries, and dropped both the radio and its batteries into the saddlebag on the side of the ATV where he had strapped the rifle.

Always avoid littering, he thought. Then he looked at the two men duct-taped to the trees and shook his head. He'd let someone else take care of picking up the rest of the rubbish.

It took a few tries because the motor had been flooded, but he got the ATV started. Half an hour later, he was on the reserve. The sight of its buildings and paved streets and the motor vehicles looked strange to him after his time in the woods. The engines, people's voices, radios, phones, and all the other sounds of so-called civilization were even stranger.

It was easy enough to find the Tribal Police building. The cop cars outside the wide log-cabin structure and the big sign made it a no-brainer. Nick parked the ATV, picked up the briefcase, climbed the steps, and walked in the open door.

The man behind the desk looked up at him and did a double take.

"Holy cow!" he said, holding up a sheet of paper with Nick's picture on it. "You're that kid who was lost."

Nick shook his head. "Nope," he said. "I'm found."

Joseph Bruchac is a writer, storyteller, proud Nulhegan Abenaki citizen, and respected elder among his people. He lives in the Adirondack mountain foothills town of Greenfield Center, New York, in the same house where his maternal grandparents raised him. Much of his writing draws on that land and his Native American ancestry. Although his northeastern American Indian heritage is only one part of an ethnic background that includes Slovak and English blood, those Native roots are the ones by which he has been most nourished. He works extensively on projects involving the preservation of Abenaki culture, language, and traditional Native skills, including performing traditional and contemporary Abenaki music with the Dawnland Singers. He is the author of more than 140 books for children and adults. He discusses Native culture and his books and presents storytelling programs at dozens of elementary and secondary schools each year as a visiting author. For more information, visit josephbruchac.com.

PathFinders novels offer exciting contemporary and historical stories featuring Native teens and written by Native authors. For more information, visit: NativeVoicesBooks.com

Walking Two Worlds

paperback • 978-1-939053-10-7 • $9.95
hardback • 978-1-939053-13-8 • $16.95

The Long Run

978-1-939053-09-1 • $9.95

Available from your local bookstore or directly from:

Book Publishing Company • PO Box 99 • Summertown, TN 38483 • 888-260-8458

Free shipping and handling on all book orders